ENGLISH VERSION BY SOPHIE HANNAH

WHO
WILL COMFORT
 ## TOFFLE?

a tale of Moomin Valley

BY TOVE JANSSON

Who lives inside this little house? It's **Toffle** all alone.
Poor **Toffle** doesn't notice quite how lonely he has grown
Outside he hears the Groke's shrill howl, Hemulen's heavy tread,
As nervously he lights his lamps to guide his way to bed.
Around him forest creatures close their doors against the night
And keep each other safe from harm with smiles and warmth and light,
But **Toffle**'s feeling cold and sad, with no companion near.
He burrows under bedclothes, body shivering with fear,
So WHO will comfort **Toffle**, tell him, 'Hush now, it's okay.
Life's bound to seem much brighter when tomorrow comes your way.'

Next morning in the foggy grey, before the sun comes out
Toffle decides to step outdoors and have a peek about.
He made it through the night but he would rather eat his hat
For breakfast every day than spend another night like that.
He packs his case and runs headfirst into the misty gloom
Then looking back he sees that all the lamps inside his room
Are burning low. When Toffle left, he didn't close his door
And now he groans to think of raindrops dripping on his floor,
But WHO will comfort Toffle, for in fact a happy band
Of fellow toffles moved straight in and took the place in hand.

So **Toffle** walks for miles until he sees a crowd of folk
All laughing with each other, taking time to share a joke,
But no-one spots poor **Toffle** and he guesses with dismay
That nobody will notice him or even look his way.
He watches from the shadows as four fillyjonks scoot past
And eight contented whompses, each more jolly than the last,
Mymble and My with daisy chains - they're all in party mood.
Toffle could go and talk to them; no-one would think him rude
But WHO will comfort **Toffle**? Who will tell him 'In the end
If all you do is hide away, you'll never find a friend.'

A few miles further on and **Toffle**'s shoes begin to pinch.
His feet are sore and tired. He cannot move another inch.
He parks his trusty suitcase underneath the sun's bright glare.
'What a relief,' thinks **Toffle**, 'that I've got a comfy chair.'
And as he sits, soft music floods his ears from far away
Where Snufkin plays his silver flute in summer's sleepy bay.
Snufkin has never had a heavy load or painful feet,
He wanders through green fields of flowers. His life must be a treat.
But WHO will comfort **Toffle** and persuade him that a song
Is better than a suitcase when the road is hard and long?

So *Toffle* trudges westwards, though in fact he doesn't know
Where he'll end up or what to do or where on earth to go
And as he tiptoes through the woods, he hears the sound of bells
And spots some merry whompses spinning round on carousels,
Dancers with flowers on their tails and lights as bright as moons
And heaps of pancakes stuffed with jam, and cakes, and macaroons,
While Hemulen lights fireworks near the tall umbrella trees.
How lonely it must feel to be a *Toffle* no-one sees,
So WHO will comfort *Toffle* and explain the way things go?
They'd know that he was there if he would only say hello.

Toffle picks up his case and makes his way towards the beach.
He sees a big white shell. What luck – it's just within his reach!
He pulls his shoes off, feels his toes sink into soft white sand
As he admires the pale blue sky, the sea, the rippling land.
'How wonderful,' thinks **Toffle**, 'I can rest, or dance or shout
Or fill my hat with pebbles.' Even so, he can't work out
Why he is still not happy. There is no-one in his way,
No Hemulen or Groke nearby. He ought to feel okay.
So WHO will comfort **Toffle** and remind him that a shell
Is nicer when there's somebody to show it to as well?

Tove

In shallow water near the shore, mysteries are afloat.
Toffle can see a bottle and inside it there's a note.
He paddles out to rescue it, to see what it might say.
If it was signed, the sea has washed its signature away,
But Toffle has the moon which is the perfect reading lamp.
He'll try to work it out, although the words are blurred and damp.
He reads aloud, 'I'm terrified! Won't someone come and help?
Won't somebody protect me when the Groke begins to yelp?
If you are strong and wise and brave, please will you call or write?
I'm just a little Miffle and it's very nearly night.'

Toffle can't bear to think of it – a girl, alone and sad.
His heart beats fast. This letter is the first he's ever had.
He folds it carefully in half and keeps it near his chest,
Feeling as if it's meant for him (though it was not addressed).
He leaves his hat and shoes behind and takes a gentle dip –
Only a small one, though. 'This sea's too cold without a ship,'
Toffle decides. He empties out the pebbles from his case,
Then climbs inside and rows away, keeping a steady pace.
The moonlight winks and **Toffle** thinks, 'I'm happy. Yes, indeed!
I know a **Miffle** needs me and a **Miffle's** all I need!'

So **Toffle** sails past three black whales, each with a water spout.
The sky is grey - a gloomy day. **Toffle** hears someone shout,
'By Jove, I'm cold!' It's Hemulen. His voice is hoarse and gruff.
Inside his rubber ring he wriggles. 'Brrr ! I've had enough!'
And **Toffle** says quite shyly, 'I am absolutely sure,
If you'll excuse my saying so, that we have met before.'
Fillijonk, in her party frock, waves as she floats nearby.
Nine whompses pass in six blue boats, and number five says 'Hi.'
'I should reply,' thinks **Toffle**. 'Since she said hello to me,
But WHO will comfort **miffle** if I dawdle endlessly?'

The Groke's black mountain hide-away looms over **Toffle**'s head.
'I think I'll visit Booble, where his fishing net is spread,'
Says **Toffle**. 'But I'd best be quick and not get in the way
Of Booble and his friends the Whompses on their holiday.
Excuse me, Booble, but has **Miffle** passed your fishing rod?'
'Yes, I believe she has,' says Booble. 'It was rather odd.
She flew past in a panic, just a day or so ago
And as for where she ended up, well, only Groke would know.
Toffle, I'd love to have you spend the afternoon with me,
But WHO will comfort **Miffle** if you linger by the sea?'

Night falls as **Toffle** wanders through a forest where the swarms
Of bats all shake their wings at him, and little furry forms
Of creatures brush against his legs, and pairs of peering eyes
Stare from among the tree trunks. He hears whispers, growls and cries
And though he's very frightened, **Toffle** knows he must be brave
There is a frightened **Miffle** that he simply has to save.
He dives inside the nearest hole as Groke begins to shriek
But makes himself climb out again. 'How can I be so weak?'
He stamps an angry foot. At last, rage has replaced his fear.
Scared **Miffles** need brave **Toffle**s when the frightful Grokes appear.

What is this dark and silent place? Is it the Groke's black yard?
Yes, if the moon is hiding and the ground is frozen hard.
And here's the Groke with yellow eyes - a fierce and awful sight,
Chilling the air around her, turning afternoon to night.
Toffle is very nervous. If he makes a small mistake
His plan might fail. He knows it has to work, for Miffle's sake.
Toffle begins his battle dance and hopes that he can win.
When Groke is least expecting it, he bites her on the shin.
Groke howls and runs away. Poor Miffle, always quick to scare,
Is even quicker to console, now Groke's no longer there.

Now *Toffle* looks at *Miffle*. They exchange a timid smile
That says as much as words, perhaps, but only for a while
Since there are certain things that even smiles cannot express.
'I'll write to you instead,' says *Toffle*, 'That's the answer. Yes!'
But when he tries to write about how lonely he has been,
About his house and Hemulen, the smooth white shell he's seen,
The Groke, the night he sailed the sea, he finds no words will come.
He is too shy to write his tale. Poor *Toffle* is struck dumb.
So WHO will comfort *Toffle* now? Will someone lend a hand
And help him write to *Miffle* so that she can understand?

(Find some writing paper. You won't need a stamp.
Just stick the letter on a rosebush where you're
sure *Miffle* will see it.)

When **miffle** reads the letter (which she finds a little tough;
Toffle's peculiar signature is difficult enough.)
Her roses turn from white to red, right before **miffle**'s eyes.
miffle falls into **Toffle**'s arms, gives him a hug and cries,
'Forget the past and all your fears. Think of the super fun
That we can have. I'd love to see the beach, a shell, the sun.'
So off they sail, two special guests on Fillyjonk's red boat.
The whompses wave and cheer to see the happy pair afloat,
And **miffle** knows, and **Toffle** knows, that both have seen the end
Of fear and fright and long, dark night, now each has found a friend.

...here are **Toffle** and **Miffle** living happily ever after.

THE END